Little Tige

"Good morning," Molly
something to do."

"Something exciting," Mrs. Jansen added.

"Good morning," the young man said. "My name is Michael. Let's see what I can find for you."

Michael turned and took a folder from the rack. "How about going up in a hot air balloon?"

Mr. Jansen looked at the folder and said, "These balloons go pretty high up. How about something less exciting?"

Mrs. Jansen looked at the folder and added, "And less expensive."

"Excuse me. Excuse me," an old woman said. She pushed ahead of Aunt Molly. She put her hands on the desk. "Excuse me," she said again.

"You're next," Michael told her.

The woman was very upset.

"I can't wait to be next," she said. "It's Little Tiger! It's Little Tiger! I'm sure something terrible has happened to my Little Tiger."

The Cam Jansen Adventure Series

DON'T FORGET ABOUT THE YOUNG CAM JANSEN
SERIES FOR YOUNGER READERS!

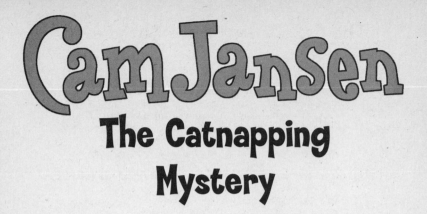

Cam Jansen

The Catnapping
Mystery

David A. Adler
Illustrated by Susanna Natti

PUFFIN BOOKS

PUFFIN BOOKS

Published by the Penguin Group

Penguin Young Readers Group, 345 Hudson Street, New York, New York 10014, U.S.A.

Penguin Group (Canada), 10 Alcorn Avenue, Toronto, Ontario, Canada M4V 3B2
(a division of Pearson Penguin Canada Inc.)

Penguin Books Ltd, 80 Strand, London WC2R 0RL, England

Penguin Ireland, 25 St Stephen's Green, Dublin 2, Ireland
(a division of Penguin Books Ltd)

Penguin Group (Australia), 250 Camberwell Road, Camberwell, Victoria 3124, Australia (a
division of Pearson Australia Group Pty Ltd)

Penguin Books India Pvt Ltd, 11 Community Centre, Panchsheel Park,
New Delhi - 110 017, India

Penguin Group (NZ), Cnr Airborne and Rosedale Roads, Albany, Auckland,
New Zealand (a division of Pearson New Zealand Ltd)

Penguin Books (South Africa) (Pty) Ltd, 24 Sturdee Avenue, Rosebank,
Johannesburg 2196, South Africa

Registered Offices: Penguin Books Ltd, 80 Strand, London WC2R 0RL, England

First published in the United States of America by Viking,
a member of Penguin Putnam Books for Young Readers, 1998
Published by Puffin Books, a division of Penguin Young Readers Group, 2000, 2005

1 3 5 7 9 10 8 6 4 2

THE LIBRARY OF CONGRESS HAS CATALOGED THE VIKING EDITION AS FOLLOWS:
Adler, David A.
Cam Jansen and the catnapping mystery / David A. Adler ; illustrated by Susanna Natti.
p. cm.— (A Cam Jansen adventure ; 18)
Summary: While visiting Aunt Molly at a fancy downtown hotel, Cam uses her
photographic memory to help one of the guests find her stolen luggage and
pet cat, and to catch the thief.
ISBN 0-670-88044-2 (hardcover)
[1. Robbers and outlaws—Fiction. 2. Hotels, motels, etc.—Fiction. 3. Mystery and detec-
tive stories.]
I. Natti, Susanna, ill. II. Title. III. Series: Adler, David A. Cam Jansen adventure;18.
PZ7.A2615Cam 1998
[Fic]—dc21
97-50544 CIP AC

Puffin Books ISBN 0-14-240289-3

Printed in the United States of America

RL: 1.9

For my great-nieces
Rivka and Devorah

Chapter One

"Yuma," Cam Jansen said. "It's a city in Arizona."

"Yuma ends with an *a*," Cam's friend Eric Shelton said. "Now I have to name a place that begins with an *a*."

Cam and Eric were walking through a busy city street with Cam's parents. They were on their way to meet Cam's Aunt Molly. While they walked, Cam and Eric were playing Geography.

"Atlanta," Eric said. "That's a city, too. It's

in Georgia." Eric smiled. "Atlanta ends with an *a.* It's our sixth *a.* I'll bet you're stuck."

Cam closed her eyes and said, "*Click.*" Cam always says, "*Click*" when she wants to remember something.

"Wait! Wait!" an old man called to his dog, which tugged at its leash. But the dog ran ahead.

The dog ran alongside Cam.

"Stop! Stop!" the old man called.

The dog stopped. It turned and looked at the old man. Then it turned and ran around Cam. The dog's leash wrapped around her. And the old man bumped into her.

Cam opened her eyes.

"It was my fault," the old man said. He unwrapped the dog's leash. "And Oliver's fault. We're both sorry."

Ruff ruff! the dog barked, and ran ahead.

"Wait, Oliver! Wait!" the old man called to the dog. But the dog didn't wait, and the old man had to run to keep up with him.

"Stop playing with dogs," Mr. Jansen told Cam.

"Dad," Cam said and smiled. "You know I'm not playing with dogs. I'm playing Geography and I need an *a*."

Cam closed her eyes again and said, "*Click*."

Then she said to Eric, "I'm not stuck. I know lots of places beginning with the letter *a*. There's Alaska, Arkansas, Ann Arbor, Altoona, Albany, Alton, Allentown, and Akron."

Cam smiled. "I have a picture in my head of a map of the United States. I'm looking at it."

Cam rubbed her chin and said, "Akron. It's a big city in Ohio. Now you have to name a place that begins with an *n*."

Cam has what people call a "photographic memory." It's as if she has a camera in her head and pictures of just about everything she has seen. Cam says "*Click*" when she wants to remember something. She says it's the sound her mental camera makes.

Cam's real name is Jennifer, but when people found out about her amazing memory, they began calling her "The Camera." Soon "The Camera" was shortened to "Cam."

Cam's eyes were still closed.

A woman wearing a purple hat with a large brim, and carrying a large bundle, bumped into her. "Excuse me," the woman said, as she walked past.

"Please, open your eyes and look where you're going," Mrs. Jansen said to Cam.

Cam opened her eyes.

"This city is so exciting," Mrs. Jansen said. "Please keep your eyes open and look at the tall buildings and all the people rushing around."

Cam looked up. She saw a few pigeons resting on a high ledge. She also saw a helicopter landing on the flat roof of a tall building.

"Please help me find the Royal Hotel," her father said. "I think it's on the next block."

"Yes! Look!" Mrs. Jansen said, and pointed. "We must be near the hotel. There's a bell-hop."

Cam and Eric looked across the street. A man in a blue uniform with gold trim was pushing a cart loaded with luggage.

The traffic light turned to red. Cam, Eric, and Cam's parents waited at the corner for the traffic light to change again. While they

waited, they watched the bellhop put the luggage into a green van.

A very long white car drove past. It turned onto a circular driveway under a red canopy with gold stripes. The driveway was jammed with taxi cabs and other cars.

"That must be the Royal," Mr. Jansen said. "It's the only hotel on this street."

The light turned green. Cam, Eric, and Cam's parents crossed the street. They walked under the canopy. A man in a red uniform, wearing a red cap, opened a large glass door.

"Welcome to the Royal," he said.

Chapter Two

The lobby was crowded. People were standing with their luggage by the long front desk. People were sitting on chairs and couches. There was a red piano on a platform, and a woman in a long black dress was playing it.

Mr. and Mrs. Jansen looked for Aunt Molly. Then, after a long while, Mr. Jansen called, "Molly! Molly!" He waved to a woman sitting by a large potted palm tree.

Aunt Molly looked across the lobby, right at Cam, Eric, and Cam's parents. Then she looked at the people sitting on the couch next to Mr. Jansen. She turned and looked at the woman playing the piano. Then she looked at the palm tree and smiled.

"No, over here," Mr. Jansen called as he walked toward Aunt Molly.

Cam, Eric, and Mrs. Jansen followed him.

"Oh, what a surprise seeing you here," Aunt Molly said. She waved her hands in front of Mr. Jansen and said, "But I can't talk to you right now. Someone is calling my name."

"That was me," Mr. Jansen told her.

"It was?" Molly asked. "Oh, of course it was," she said. She hugged Mr. and Mrs. Jansen.

"Oh, my," she said when she looked at Cam. "You and your friend Sheldon are getting so big."

"Molly," Mr. Jansen said, "his name is Eric Shelton, not Sheldon."

"Is that right?" Aunt Molly asked Eric.

Eric nodded.

Molly put her hand to her cheek, shook her head, and asked, "Are you sure?"

"Yes, he's sure," Mr. Jansen told her.

"What have you planned for us?" Mrs. Jansen asked. "You said you would find something exciting for us to do."

"Did I?" Molly asked. "I'm a little confused. I've been doing so much traveling. You know," she said to Eric, "I work for an airline. I just came from New Orleans."

"New Orleans!" Eric said. "That begins with an *n*. That's my answer," he told Cam. "Now you need a place that begins with an *s*."

Cam told Molly, "We're playing Geography."

"That's nice," Molly said. "And thank you," she told Mr. Jansen. "I had such a nice time with you today."

"Molly," Mr. Jansen said very slowly. "We just got here. We haven't done anything yet."

"Oh, my," Aunt Molly said. "That's right." She smiled. "I am *very* confused today."

She started across the lobby. Then she turned and said, "Come with me."

Aunt Molly led them to a young man at one end of the front desk. Behind him was a rack with folders describing things to do in the city.

"Good morning," Molly said. "We're looking for something to do."

"Something exciting," Mrs. Jansen added.

"Good morning," the young man said. "My
name is Michael. Let's see what I can find for
you."

Michael turned and took a folder from the
rack. "How about going up in a hot air balloon?"

Mr. Jansen looked at the folder and said, "These balloons go pretty high up. How about something less exciting?"

Mrs. Jansen looked at the folder and added, "And less expensive."

"Excuse me. Excuse me," an old woman said. She pushed ahead of Aunt Molly. She put her hands on the desk. "Excuse me," she said again.

"You're next," Michael told her.

The woman was very upset.

"I can't wait to be next," she said. "It's Little Tiger! It's Little Tiger! I'm sure something terrible has happened to my Little Tiger."

Chapter Three

"You have a tiger?" Eric asked.

Mrs. Jansen patted the woman's hand and said, "Just take a deep breath and tell us what happened."

The woman took a deep breath.

"Did you hear that?" Eric whispered to Cam. "She has a tiger."

"Maybe it's one of those toy stuffed animals," Cam whispered.

"Oh, no," the woman said and took another breath. "My Little Tiger is real. And she's such a dear. I take her everywhere."

15

"This is exciting," Mrs. Jansen said.

"I came to the hotel," the woman told Michael. "I arrived by taxi. The circle drive in front was filled with cars. The driver said, 'I can't get in there. How about I leave you off here?'"

The woman put her hand to her chest and took another deep breath.

Then she said, "Well, he didn't even wait for me to answer. He stopped the car and got out. He opened the trunk and took out my luggage. There I was, standing on the sidewalk with two big suitcases and my Little Tiger. I couldn't carry all that!"

The woman turned and said to Aunt Molly, "Those bags are heavy."

Molly nodded. "I try to get everything into one suitcase. And it has wheels."

"Well," the woman said. "I was lucky. A nice young man, a bellhop, came to the sidewalk and said, 'I'll take that.'

"I wasn't sure pets are allowed in the hotel. The bellhop said he would take everything straight to my room. So I gave him Little Tiger, too.

"Well, I've waited in my room for a long time and he hasn't brought me my Little Tiger, and he hasn't brought me my bags. I'm worried."

"Don't worry," Michael told her. He rang a bell. "We'll find your luggage."

A bellhop rushed to the front desk. On the front of his red uniform was a badge with the name "Greg" on it.

He looked around. Then he asked Michael, "Who needs help with luggage?"

"A while ago, this woman gave her luggage to one of the bellhops," Michael said. "She's still waiting for it."

Greg took out a small pad and asked the woman, "What's your name and room number?"

18

"My name is Mrs. Esther Wright," the woman told him. "That's Wright with a *w*. I'm in room 613."

"I'll take care of it," Greg said.

"Oh, this is so exciting," Molly said. "Imagine, a real tiger loose in a big hotel."

"Aren't you afraid your tiger will bite you?" Eric asked.

"Oh, no," Esther Wright answered. "My Little Tiger is such a sweet and gentle little cat."

"Little cat!" Cam, Eric, Mr. and Mrs. Jansen, Aunt Molly, and Michael all said.

"Tigers are not *little* cats," Eric told Mrs. Wright. "Tigers are *big* cats."

"Well," Esther Wright said. She held her hands about one foot apart and said, "She's only about this big."

She laughed. "She's not a real tiger. She's a cat. She has stripes, so I *named* her Little Tiger."

"Oh," Eric said.

They all waited by Michael's end of the desk. They watched Greg talk to the other bellhops. Then Greg went into a room behind the front desk. He came out a short while later and walked quickly to Esther Wright.

"I checked with my boss, the bell captain," he told her. "Then I checked the luggage room. I couldn't find your things."

Chapter Four

"**W**hat!" Mrs. Wright cried out. "My Little Tiger is gone! And all my clothing and jewelry!"

"I didn't say they were gone," Greg told her quickly. "I said I didn't find them."

"I think they're gone," Cam whispered.

"Don't worry," Molly told Esther Wright. "I've lost my luggage lots of times. Once, I bought a newspaper and chewing gum in an airport. I left my suitcase by one of the magazine racks. I think that was in San Diego."

"San Diego," Cam whispered to Eric. "That begins with an *s* and that's my answer. Now you need a place that begins with an *o*."

"Um," Eric said.

"I didn't lose my Little Tiger or my luggage," Esther Wright declared. "I gave them to a bellhop."

"Well," Greg said. "Maybe the bellhop took everything to the wrong room."

Greg looked across the lobby. Then he said, "This is a big hotel. We have a lot of bellhops here. Do you know the name of the one who took your things?"

"No," Mrs. Wright said, and looked around. "But when I see him, I'll know him."

Greg said, "Please, come with me."

Cam, Eric, and the others watched Esther Wright and Greg walk to the bellhop's desk. Greg's boss was sitting behind the desk. Two other bellhops were standing there. Esther Wright looked at them both and shook her head. Neither one had taken her luggage.

Molly laughed. "Once I waited and waited for my luggage to come off the airplane," she said. "And do you know what? I had never put it on the airplane. I forgot it at home."

"Don't worry," Michael said. "She'll get her luggage. Now I have to find you something exciting to do."

He turned and took three folders from the rack.

"You could take a helicopter ride over the city. Or, you could take a horse and buggy ride. And of course, the Kurt Daub Museum is near the hotel. There are lots of great things to see and do there."

Mr. and Mrs. Jansen looked at the folders. Cam, Eric, and Aunt Molly watched what was happening at the bellhop's desk.

There was a telephone on the desk. Whenever it rang, the bell captain picked it up. He listened and then told one of the bellhops where to go to help someone in the hotel. Bellhops who were done carrying luggage came back to the desk and waited for something else to do.

Cam, Eric, and Aunt Molly saw Esther Wright shake her head each time another bellhop came to the desk. None of them was the one who had taken her things.

"Let's go to the museum," Mr. Jansen said.

"I'm sure we'll have fun there. And maybe we'll learn something."

Ring! Ring!

The telephone on the bell captain's desk rang. The bell captain picked it up. He spoke into it. He listened and then gave the telephone to Mrs. Wright.

She listened. Then she dropped the telephone and cried out loud, "My baby! My Little Tiger! My Little Tiger!"

Chapter Five

Cam ran to her. "What happened? What happened to your cat?" Cam asked.

Greg and the bell captain leaned forward to listen. Eric, Mr. and Mrs. Jansen, and Aunt Molly had followed Cam. They were listening, too.

"That was the bellhop on the telephone," Esther Wright said. She wiped a tear from her eye and sobbed. "No. It was the thief."

"Don't say that," the bell captain told Mrs. Wright. "The people who work for me are not thieves."

"He said he has my luggage. He went
through it. He said my clothing is old. The
jewelry is fake."

Esther Wright wiped away another tear.
Then she went on. "And he said, 'And then
there's the cat. The only person I could sell
this stuff to is you. So go to your room and
wait there. Wait there alone. I'll call and tell
you what to do.'"

"Oh, my," Aunt Molly said. "This is terrible."

"You must call the police," Mr. Jansen said. "This is a kidnapping." He thought for a moment and then said, "No. It's a catnapping."

Greg took the telephone and called the police.

Mrs. Jansen brought a chair. Esther Wright sat and rested her head in her hands.

"The thief must be a bellhop from another shift," the bell captain said. He looked through his desk. "I have a picture here of most of them, from a party we had."

"A picture!" Cam said. "Of course! I have lots of pictures."

Cam closed her eyes and said, "*Click*."

"What should I do?" Esther Wright asked.

Greg gave her the telephone. "It's the police sergeant," Greg said. "He wants to speak with you."

The bell captain gave Esther Wright a photograph and said, "Look at this. See if you can find the thief."

"This is too much for me," Mrs. Wright said. "I can't do everything."

Mrs. Jansen took the telephone. She spoke to the police sergeant. Esther Wright looked at the photograph.

Cam opened her eyes. She looked at Greg and the bell captain. Then she closed her eyes again and said, "*Click.*"

Esther Wright gave the photograph back to the bell captain and said, "None of these is the thief."

Mrs. Jansen hung up the telephone. "Two police officers will be here soon," she told Esther Wright. "They'll wait with you for the next call from the thief."

Esther Wright rested her head in her hands again and said, "My poor Little Tiger."

Someone pulled two large suitcases on wheels to the desk. He told Greg his room

number. Greg put the bags on a cart and pushed it toward the elevator.

A few people had gathered in the center of the lobby. The woman in the long black dress was still playing the piano. People were singing.

Two tall police officers came through the front door. One was a woman with short black hair. The other was a man with a droopy mustache. They walked over to the bell captain's desk.

"I'm Officer Johnson and this is my partner, Officer Goldberg," the woman said. "Now whose luggage was stolen?"

Esther Wright looked up and said, "Mine. And my pet cat, Little Tiger, too!"

Cam opened her eyes.

"Don't worry," Officer Johnson said. "We'll catch the thief."

"And we'll save your cat," the other officer said.

"And I can help," Cam told them. "I can help."

Chapter Six

"Let's go," Officer Johnson said. "We'll wait in your room for the thief to call."

Esther Wright told the officers, "But he said I should wait there alone."

"When he calls," Officer Goldberg said, "we'll be very quiet. He won't even know we're there."

The two police officers and Esther Wright went toward the elevator. Cam followed them.

"I can help," Cam said again when they reached the elevators.

Officer Johnson pressed the elevator button and the door opened. She, Officer Goldberg, and Esther Wright got into the elevator. Then Officer Johnson turned and told Cam, "We're busy now."

Cam stepped into the elevator just as its door was closing.

Esther Wright pressed the button for the sixth floor.

"I told you we're busy now," Officer Johnson said sharply to Cam. "As soon as we get to the sixth floor, you'll have to go right down again."

"But I can help!" Cam said again.

Cam closed her eyes and said, "*Click.*"

Then she asked Esther Wright, "Was the bellhop who took your luggage about as tall as Officer Goldberg?"

Esther Wright looked at Officer Goldberg.

"Yes," Esther Wright told Cam.

"Did he have long brown hair? Were there three gold earrings in his left ear?" Cam asked.

"Yes," Esther Wright said again.

"How do you know so much about the thief?" Officer Johnson asked.

The door of the elevator opened.

"Come with us," Officer Johnson told Cam.

They all followed Mrs. Wright to room 613. She took out her key and opened the door. Esther Wright and the two police officers sat on the bed, right by the telephone.

"Well," Officer Johnson asked Cam. "How do you know so much about the thief?"

"When we were coming here," Cam explained, "my mom saw a bellhop. He was putting luggage in a green van. That's how we knew we were near the Royal Hotel. But he was not one of the hotel's bellhops. We should have known that as soon as we came in here. I should have known then that something strange was going on."

"Why?" Officer Goldberg asked.

Cam said, "Because his jacket and little cap were *blue*. The bellhops and the doorman

here all wear *red* uniforms. Even the front canopy is red."

"That's right," Esther Wright said. "Everything here is red. The bellhop who took my things *was* wearing a blue uniform."

Knock! Knock!

Someone was at the door. Officer Johnson opened it.

Mr. and Mrs. Jansen, Aunt Molly, and Eric came into the room "There you are," Mrs. Jansen said when she saw Cam. "You must not run off like that."

Ring! Ring!

The telephone was ringing. Esther Wright reached for it.

Officer Johnson held up her hand. "Quiet, please," she said. "This might be the thief."

Ring! Ring!

Esther Wright picked up the telephone and said, "Hello."

Chapter Seven

Esther Wright listened. Then she said, "Yes, I understand. I'll do whatever you tell me to do. I just want my Little Tiger back."

She hung up the telephone.

"Well, what did he say?" Officer Johnson asked.

"He wants five thousand dollars wrapped in an old newspaper. In exactly two hours, I have to leave it behind the third column to the right of the front entrance to the Kurt Daub Museum. Once he gets the money, he'll call here and tell me where to find Little Tiger and my things."

"Why don't you try to trace his next call?" Mrs. Jansen asked.

"No," Officer Goldberg told her. "He doesn't stay on the telephone long enough for that."

Esther Wright looked at her watch as she got up from the bed. "I'll pay the money.

That's what I'll do. I'll pay the money and get Little Tiger back."

"Maybe I can help you find the thief," Cam told Officer Johnson. "I saw him and his van."

Esther Wright was at the door. "I have to hurry. I have just two hours to deliver the money," she said as she left the room.

Eric told the police officers, "Cam has solved lots of mysteries and caught lots of thieves."

"Well," Officer Johnson asked Cam, "how can you help us find the thief?"

Cam closed her eyes and said, "*Click!*"

"What's she doing?" Officer Goldberg asked.

"That helps her remember," Mrs. Jansen whispered.

"The thief loaded the luggage into a green van," Cam said. "There was a lot of mud on the van."

"Did you see the license plate?" Officer Johnson asked.

"No," Cam answered. "But I did see something else. Our car has only two decals on the front windshield. But I saw three on the van."

"One is the registration sticker," Officer Goldberg said. "One is the inspection sticker. Now, tell us about the third one."

"It was round and near the top of the window. Across it were three curved stripes, blue, red, and green, like a rainbow," Cam said with her eyes still closed. "And there was the outline of a leaf and a number."

"That's from the garage at the Oak Tree Apartments," Officer Johnson said. "Maybe the thief lives there. I know Beth, the garage woman. If we find the van, she'll tell us who owns it."

Officer Goldberg said, "Let's go. We have to hurry."

The two police officers left the room. Cam, Eric, Mr. Jansen, Mrs. Jansen, and Aunt Molly followed them. They all got into the elevator.

"Where are all of you going?" Officer Johnson asked.

"You need me," Cam said, "to show you the van."

"And we're her parents," Mr. and Mrs. Jansen said together.

"And I'm her Aunt Molly. I work for an airline."

Eric looked up at Officer Johnson and smiled. "And I'm only ten years old," he said. "I can't be left here alone."

The elevator door opened.

"We need the *click* girl," Officer Johnson said. "Whoever else fits in the back seat of our car is welcome to come."

"Let's go," Officer Goldberg said. "We have to hurry."

Chapter Eight

The lobby was still crowded. The woman in the long black dress was playing a popular song on the red piano. Lots of people were singing.

The police officers, Cam, and the others rushed past the red piano. The woman stopped playing as they went past.

"Hey," the bell captain called as they passed his desk. "Did you catch the thief?"

"We will," Officer Johnson said.

The police car was parked just outside the hotel entrance. Officer Johnson got in the driver's seat. Officer Goldberg got in the passenger side of the front seat. Then he opened the back door for the others.

Mrs. Jansen got in first. Then Cam got in and sat on her mother's lap. Aunt Molly went in next, followed by Mr. Jansen. Eric looked in at the crowded back seat.

"We're in a hurry," Officer Goldberg said.

Aunt Molly said, "Get in, Sheldon. There's plenty of room."

"His name is *Eric Shelton*," Mr. Jansen said as Eric squeezed in and sat on his lap.

Officer Goldberg turned on the siren and Officer Johnson drove off.

Rrrr! Rrrr!

Each time the car hit a bump, Cam's and Eric's heads hit the roof of the car.

Rrrr! Rrrr!

"This is so exciting," Molly said.

They went through a red light and sped quickly around a corner.

"Turn off the siren," Officer Johnson said. "We don't want the thief to know we're coming."

Officer Goldberg shut the siren off just as Officer Johnson turned the car onto a driveway. She drove the car into a garage beneath a large apartment building.

A woman wearing jeans and a sweatshirt came out of the garage office. She walked over to the car.

"Hi, Beth," Officer Johnson said to her. "We're looking for a green van."

"There's one right here," Beth said, and pointed. "And there are two others."

Cam and the others got out of the police car. Cam looked at the green van. She closed her eyes and said, "*Click.*" Then she opened her eyes and looked at the van again.

"This is not the one," she said. "The one near the hotel had mud on it and a large dent in the back."

"I'll show you the others," Beth said.

She led everyone through the garage to another green van. This one was parked next to a large cement pole.

Cam looked at the van. She closed her eyes and said, "*Click.*" Then she opened her eyes and said, "This is it."

The two police officers turned to Beth.

"It belongs to the man in apartment 7E," she told them.

"Thanks," Officer Goldberg said, as he and

Officer Johnson walked to the elevator in the corner of the garage.

Cam and the others followed them.

"Where are all of you going?" Officer Johnson asked when the elevator door opened.

"You'll need me to identify the thief," Cam said as she stepped into the elevator.

"And we're her parents," Mr. and Mrs. Jansen said together.

"Not this again!" Officer Johnson said. "Just get in." Then she pushed the button for the seventh floor.

The elevator went up. Then it stopped and the door opened. Everyone got off.

"Stay here," Officer Goldberg said.

The two officers went to apartment 7E. They knocked on the door and waited. They knocked again, and Officer Johnson said, "*Police*," very loudly.

The door opened.

"What is it?" the person who opened the door asked. He didn't step outside the apartment, so Cam couldn't see if he was the thief.

"We're investigating a robbery," Officer Johnson said.

The man said, "I didn't rob anyone."

"Do you mind if a girl comes here and takes a look at you?" Officer Goldberg asked.

The man said, "I didn't rob any girl."

Officer Goldberg signaled for Cam to come over.

Cam took one look at the man and said, "Yes. That's him."

Chapter Nine

"Hey," the man said. "I didn't rob her!"

Meow!

A gold and black striped cat ran out. Cam reached for it, and it ran into her hands.

"Is this your cat?" Officer Johnson asked the man.

"Yes," he answered. "I'm allowed to have a cat, aren't I?"

Cam looked at the tag around the cat's neck. "What's the cat's name?" Cam asked.

The man thought for a moment and then

answered, "It doesn't have a name. I just say, 'Here Kitty,' and it comes to me."

"The cat's name is Little Tiger," Cam said. She showed the tag to Officer Goldberg.

The man scratched his head and said, "Yes, that's right. I say 'Here, Kitty. Here, Little Tiger,' and it comes."

"Stop playing games," Officer Johnson said. "We know you stole the cat and luggage from a woman named Esther Wright. I can see the suitcases from here. They're next to your television set."

"So they're not my things," the man said. "But that woman gave them to me. Is that a crime?"

"You took her things and you held them for ransom," Officer Goldberg said. "That is a crime."

"You're under arrest," Officer Johnson told the man. She took out a printed card and read it to him.

"You have the right to remain silent," she began.

When she was done, Officer Goldberg told the man, "Come with us."

The officers watched from the door as he went to get a jacket. On his way out, he picked up two large suitcases.

"Here," he said, and gave the suitcases to

the officers. "Give her back her stuff. And give her back her cat. It scratched my chair and made a mess."

The police officers each took a suitcase. In the elevator, Officer Goldberg thanked Cam and the others for their help. Then he said, "I'm sorry, but you'll have to find your own way back to the hotel. We're taking this man to the police station."

"What about Little Tiger?" Cam asked.

Officer Goldberg said, "Bring her back to Esther Wright. And tell her to come to the police station to pick up her luggage. She has to fill out some forms."

The elevator door opened. The officers led the man to their car. Then they drove off.

Meow.

"Nice cat," Cam said, and patted Little Tiger.

Cam, her parents, Eric, and Aunt Molly went to the small garage office. Mrs. Jansen asked Beth if she could use the telephone.

"Sure," Beth said.

Mrs. Jansen took out a card with the Royal Hotel telephone number. Then she dialed.

"Mrs. Wright is in room 613," Cam told her mother. "And can I talk?"

Mrs. Jansen waited. Then she said, "Room 613," and gave the telephone to Cam.

Cam waited. But there was no answer.

"I know where she is," Eric said. "Mrs. Wright is probably waiting near the front of the Kurt Daub Museum."

Meow, Little Tiger said.

Cam hung up the telephone. Beth told them how to get to the museum.

"Oh, my," Mrs. Jansen said as they left the garage. "This is a real adventure."

"See," Aunt Molly said. "I told you we would do something exciting."

Eric walked alongside her and whispered, "Aunt Molly, do you know a place that begins with the letter *o*?"

"I left my luggage once next to a water

fountain in Ohio," Aunt Molly said. "Ohio begins with an *o*."

"Ohio," Eric said to Cam. "Ohio begins and ends with an *o*. So now you need another place that begins with an *o*."

Aunt Molly thought for a moment and then asked, "Do you know why I left my luggage next to a water fountain?"

"Were you confused again?" Mr. Jansen asked.

"Of course not," Aunt Molly said. "I was thirsty!"

When they came to the museum, they saw Esther Wright waiting. Little Tiger jumped out of Cam's arms and ran to her.

"Oh, Little Tiger! Little Tiger!" Mrs. Wright said, and hugged the cat.

"The police have the thief," Cam told Mrs. Wright.

"And they have your luggage," Eric added.

Esther Wright looked around. Then she asked, "The thief was caught?"

54

"Yes," Eric said. "Cam *click*ed and solved the mystery."

Esther Wright ran behind one of the large cement columns. She came back holding an old newspaper.

"I have my cat and my money, and I'll get my luggage," she said. "Thank you so much for your help. We should celebrate."

Mrs. Wright pointed to an outdoor restaurant. "Let's go there and all get some ice cream."

Meow, Little Tiger said.

"And some milk," Mrs. Wright said.

"And then," Mrs. Jansen said, "we can visit the Kurt Daub Museum." She sighed. "I just hope it's quiet in there. I've had enough excitement for one day."

Aunt Molly laughed. Cam, Eric, Mr. Jansen, and even Mrs. Wright laughed, too.

Cam Jansen has a photographic memory. Do you? Study the picture on page 17. Blink your eyes, say, "*Click!*" and then turn to page 58. See how much you remember.

1. How many people are pictured on page 17?

2. Which one of those people is sitting?

3. How many people are listening to the piano player's music?

4. Who is standing closest to Mrs. Esther Wright's left elbow?

5. How many folders are on the counter?

6. Is Cam's mouth open or closed?